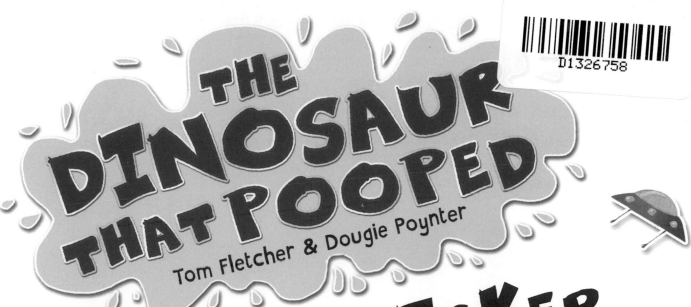

THE DINOSAUR THAT POOPED

Tom Fletcher & Dougie Poynter

SPACE STICKER ACTIVITY BOOK

Can you spot the torch on every page?

When you see brown shapes, look on your sticker sheets to find the matching sticker

RED FOX

DRESS UP DANNY AND DINOSAUR

Danny and Dinosaur are planning to go on an
awesome adventure, but first they need to get ready.
Use your stickers to help Danny get dressed.

Trace these letters to write their names.

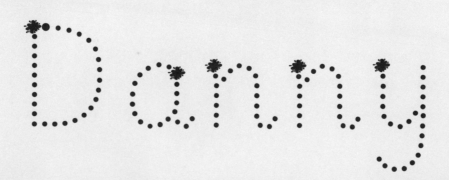

Get Dino ready by drawing him a hat, some socks and some funny glasses.

Now colour him in!

SPOT THE DIFFERENCE

Spot ten differences between these pictures.

Add a dinosaur poop sticker for each one you find!

Answers on page 24.

A FEAST FOR A BEAST

Mummy is making Danny and Dinosaur
a packed lunch for their space trip.
Find the missing food on your sticker page.

How many of these can you spot?
Trace the number in the box.

Cheese

Sausages

Tomatoes

Juice

Answers on page 24.

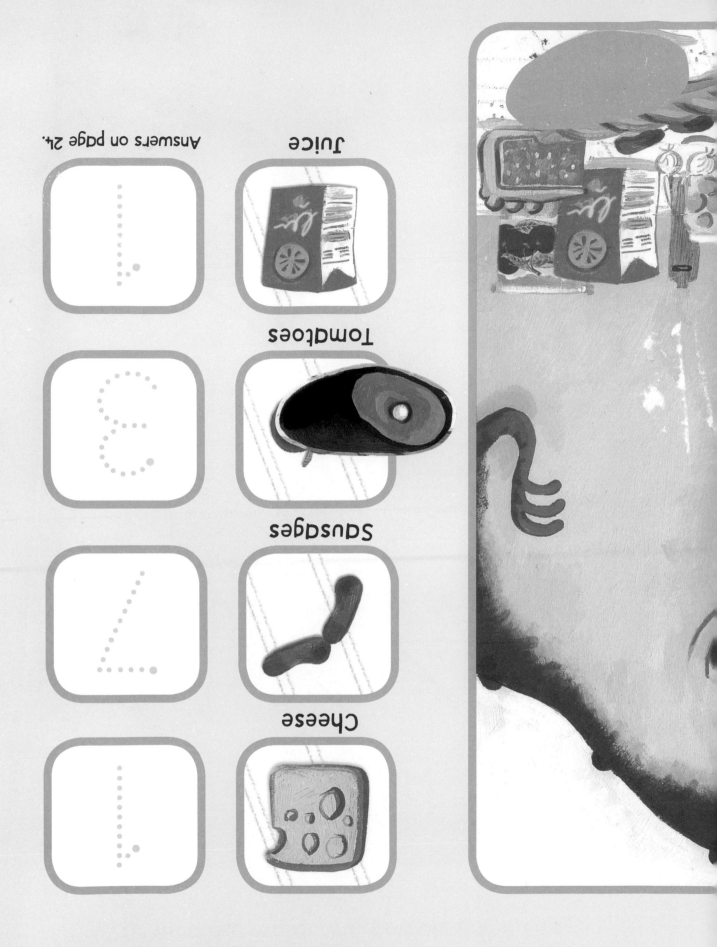

3 . . . 2 . . . 1 . . . IGNITION!

Look, Danny has found a space rocket! Join the dots using a pencil and colour it in! Then join the dots around the moon and colour in the sky.

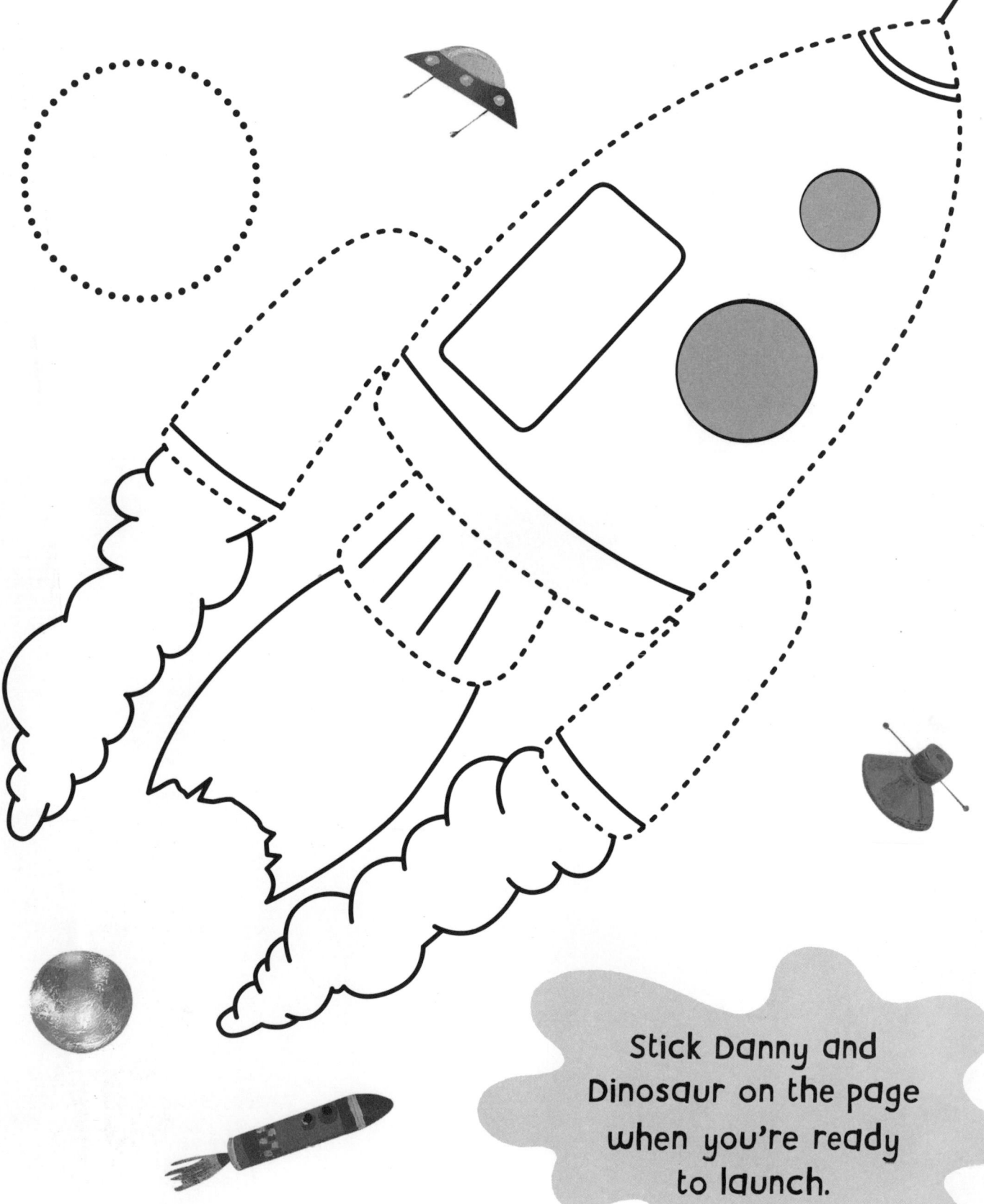

Stick Danny and Dinosaur on the page when you're ready to launch.

GINORMOUS JUMBLE

These words have got all jumbled up in Dinosaur's tummy.
Draw a line to link the mixed-up words to the right pictures.

DANNY

CRHTO ATRS

OPO RATHE

NANDY ATC

CAT

TORCH

POO

EARTH

STAR

Answers on page 24.

GOBBLEDY POOP

Dinosaur's hungry again, and he's eating everything in sight! Follow his trail and add the stickers of the things he gobbles up along the way to his tummy.

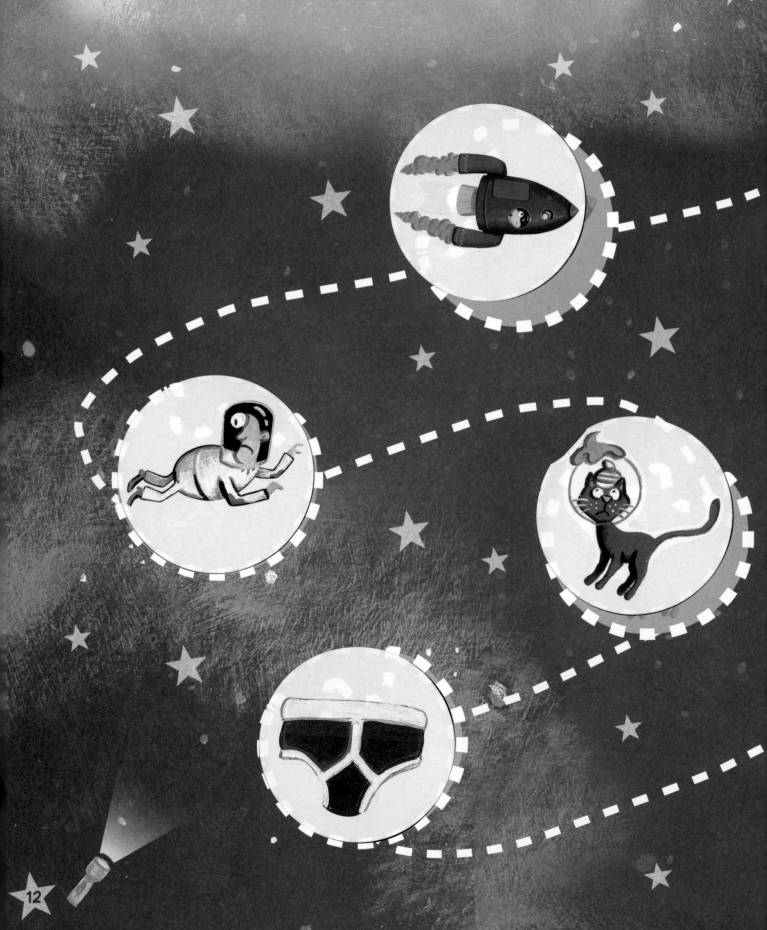

12

STINKY SCENE

Parts of this picture have been covered with something brown and smelly... Use your stickers to add the missing pieces and complete the picture.

SPACE WORDSEARCH

Can you find the hidden words in the control panel?

ROCKET   TORCH   POOP
DANNY   CHEESE   SMELLY
DINOSAUR   CAT   BUM

S	M	E	L	L	Y	C	J
B	O	Q	B	L	P	A	P
U	R	O	C	K	E	T	O
M	C	F	X	L	R	M	O
U	T	O	R	C	H	P	P
D	I	N	O	S	A	U	R
W	V	M	D	A	N	N	Y
C	H	E	E	S	E	N	F

Answers on page 24.

SUPER-POOPER IN SPACE

Oh dear! Lots of things are coming out of Dino's bottom! What else has Dinosaur pooped? Add your stickers to the page to create a super-pooper space scene!

POOP FACTS!

Did you know that a 'coprolite' is a fossilised poop? Fossilised vomit is called 'regurgitalite' – gross!

The largest dinosaur poop ever found was 17 inches long and full of animal bones. Scientists think it came from a big dinosaur like a T. rex.

There's a street in Ipswich, UK, called Coprolite Street (Old Poop Street!)
I wonder if that's where Danny lives?

POOP JOKES!

What do you call a dino who pooped a long time ago?
Ex-stinks!

What's brown and sticky?
A stick!

Knock, knock!
Who's there?
I smelp.
I smelp who?
Haha!

MESSY MAZE

Poor Danny is lost in space. Follow Dinosaur's
trail of poo to help Danny find his way home.
Avoid the piles of poop along the way.

Start

Hooray!

You're home, safe and sound!

Answer on page 24.

SEARCH FOR THE ROCKET

Silly Dinosaur has lost one of the rockets.
Follow the trails to help him find it.

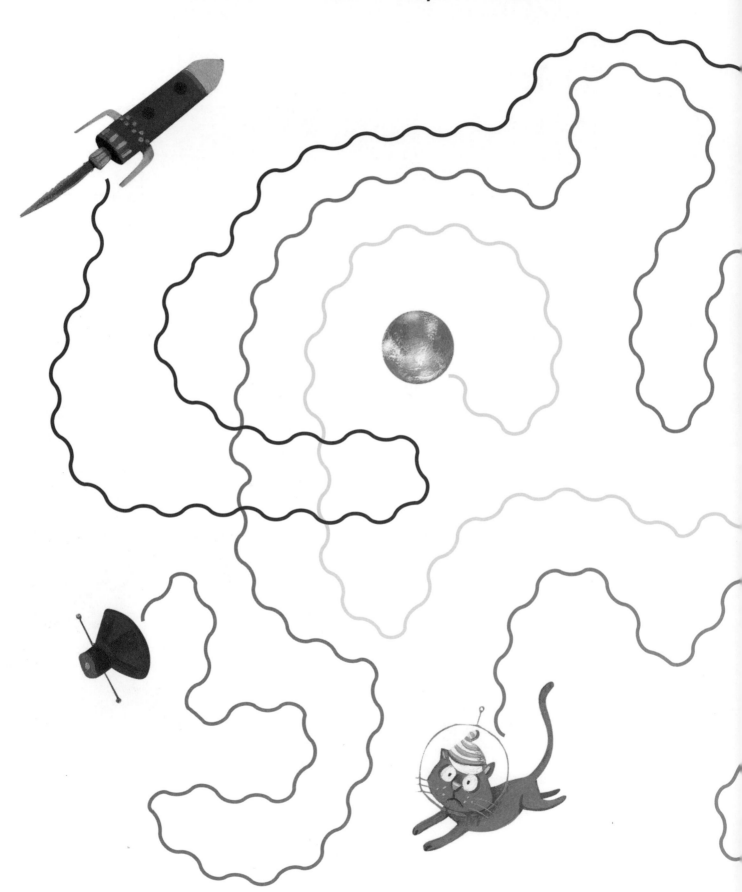

SPACE COUNTDOWN

Answers on page 24.

Rockets

Planets

Comets

Look at the list of objects below — can you find
them all? Look for the correct number from your
sticker page and add it to each box.

3

Satellites

2

Aliens

1

Moon

ANSWERS

SPOT THE DIFFERENCE Page 4-5

FEAST FOR A BEAST Page 6-7

Cheese — 1
Sausages — 7
Tomatoes — 3
Juice — 1

I SPY, IN THE SKY... Page 10

I SPY, IN THE SKY...

There are lots of things to see up in space! Count the stars and trace the number in the box, then use your stickers to decorate the sky scene. — 12

GINORMOUS JUMBLE Page 11

CRHTO — TORCH
ATRS — STAR
OPO — POO
RATHE — EARTH
NANDY — DANNY
ATC — CAT

TORCH POO EARTH STAR

SPACE WORDSEARCH Page 15

S	M	E	L	L	Y	C	J
B	O	Q	B	L	P	A	P
U	R	O	C	K	E	T	O
M	C	F	X	L	R	M	O
U	T	O	R	C	H	P	P
D	I	N	O	S	A	U	R
W	V	M	D	A	N	N	Y
C	H	E	E	S	E	N	F

MESSY MAZE Page 19

Start

Hooray!
You're home, safe and sound!
Answer on page 24.

SPACE COUNTDOWN Page 22-23

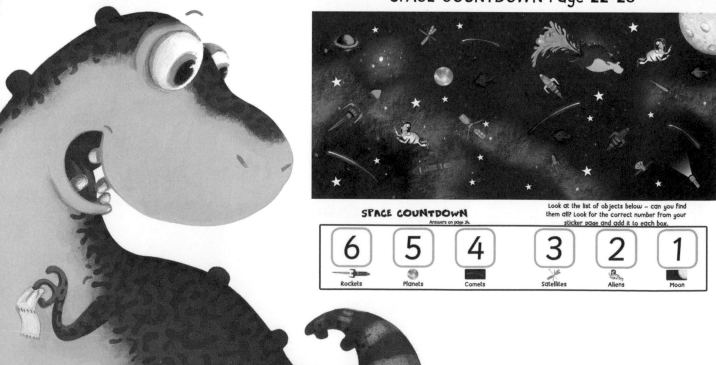

SPACE COUNTDOWN
Answers on page 24.

Look at the list of objects below – can you find them all? Look for the correct number from your sticker page and add it to each box.

6 Rockets
5 Planets
4 Comets
3 Satellites
2 Aliens
1 Moon